Elsie's Bird

Philomel
Books

An Imprint of
Penguin Group (USA) Inc.

Elsie's Bird

JANE YOLEN

illustrated by DAVID SMALL

Elsie was a Boston girl.
From the time she was a little child, hair in pigtails,
she knew the cozy harbor where gulls screamed at fishing boats,
where the fish merchants called,
"Fresh cod, fresh!"

She would run along the lazy curves
of the busy streets, listening to the clop
of horses' hooves on stone cobbles.
She played skip rope with her friends,
calling "Lady, Lady, at the gate . . ."

Birds began singing before sunrise
and Elsie knew all of their names—
cardinal, chickadee, robin, wren.
She loved to sing their songs
back at them.

But then her mama died.
After that, every Sunday, when the steeple bell rang,
Elsie went to church with her papa
to speak familiar prayers
and sing favorite hymns, and remember.
Even so, it was a comfortable childhood,
and all Elsie knew.
But Papa longed for something else,
something far away from Boston
and the sadness in his heart.

When Elsie turned eight,
Papa could no longer disguise his longing.
"We are going west, Elsie," he said.
"We are going to find some happiness
away from here."
She thought west meant Concord or Lincoln,
towns a day's travel away.
He meant someplace much further,
a faraway place called Nebraska,
where there were few people,
and almost no towns at all.

Elsie's grandmother Nana wept
and her grandfather Nonny harrumphed.
Her friends all made her little gifts.
Then Elsie and her father got on a train.
They both carried carpetbags full of clothes,
and brought along a maple chest
packed with linens her mother had sewn
over the long year before she died.
Best of all, Elsie took a birdcage
with her new canary, Timmy Tune,
yellow as the sun over Boston Harbor.
They sang to one another, bird and girl,
along the gathering miles.

All the way west, the clacketing of the wheels
reminded Elsie how far she was going,
away from the sound of the sea
and the familiar bowl of sky.
She might not have gone west
had she known the only sea there was a sea of grass.

She might not have gone west
had she known the nearest neighbors lived miles away.
She might have stayed home in Boston
with her Nana and Nonny.
But she had already lost her mother.
She couldn't bear to be parted from Papa, too.

When they got to Nebraska,
to the plot of land Papa had bought,
there was only a house built in the ground.
Its roof was made of sod,
and grass grew around the chimney.
Elsie wrote a letter home to Nana and Nonny.
"Here there is only grass and sky and silence."
The only sound at night
was her own crying in her little bed,
but she didn't let Papa know.

Sure, there was sound in Nebraska—
wind through the grass during the day,
crickets and grasshoppers at night.
But Elsie couldn't hear it.
And when it rained that hard rain,
she huddled, not listening,
in the cool dark of the sod house,
dreaming of Boston cobbles and bells.

The only familiar comfort she had
was Timmy Tune,
and she sang back and forth with him,
hymns and jump-rope tunes and old catches
and sailor songs like "Cape Cod Girls"
and "Come all ye bold fishermen."
She sang as she made dinner, or sewed a sampler.
She sang as she watched out the window
as Papa plowed with their great horse Jo.

Sometimes she stood at the door,
following Papa with her eyes as he
rode off in the wagon
to get supplies in the nearest town
ten miles away.
But she didn't go outside to wave good-bye.
Oh, Papa tried to get her to walk out.
He'd say, "Come with me to the river, Elsie,
the fish are jumping at the flies."

Or "Come out with me to see the sunset,
painting the big sky red."
But she was afraid to lose herself
in the silence of the prairie.
She would touch Timmy Tune's cage
as if he kept her safe.
"Well, I'm glad you've got that canary,"
Papa said, then hugged her and drove away.

Only one Friday—when Papa had gone off again,
buying seed corn for the coming spring—
Elsie accidentally left the cage door open.
Timmy flew right out,
winging through an open window.
Elsie grabbed up the cage
and without thinking, ran outside after him.
"Timmy!" she cried, and whistled.

"Timmy," she called, to coax him back.
She ran across the farmyard,
and into the tall prairie grass,
crying the canary's name.
"Timmy," she sobbed. "Timmy."
Until all that could be seen of her
was the hand holding the cage
up above the high grass.

The sun rose high, and higher still,
as Elsie whistled and pushed through the grass,
till the house was lost behind her.
Papa had told her a tale of a farm wife
who walked farther and farther into the sea of grass,
and never came back.
He'd meant it as a warning.
But she didn't care.
It was Timmy who was lost,
Timmy who had to be found.
"Timmy!"

She cried again,
and then—in a thin, hoarse voice—
began to sing his favorite song:
"*Go in and out the window.*"
She kept walking till
she came upon a small creek
where she sank down crying on the bank.
And there, where the grass stood green-gold,
Timmy Tune began to sing back,
circling and circling overhead.
Then, he flew down, perched on her shoulder
and sang out loud and long.
Gently, she put her hands around him,
not like a cage to keep him in,
but just to touch his golden head.

Suddenly, they both heard
a raspy *koo-a-lee koo-a-lee.*
A blackbird flew over to them and sang again.
"Koo-a-lee," Elsie sang back. *"Koo-a-lee."*
And then, oh then—sitting there
by the burbling creek,
in the green-gold grass,
under the sun-washed sky,
Elsie finally heard the voices of the plains.

She heard wind rippling the grass.
She heard long vees of geese
spinning out cries like thread;
the creaking call of sandhill cranes;
the bubbly larkspur far out over the tall stalks.
She clapped her hands
and sang back to them, too,
skip-rope songs and sea shanties
and hymns from her Boston church.
And Timmy Tune sang along with her.

"Elsie, Elsie, where are you?"
Elsie heard a frightened voice calling her name
from far, far away in the grass.
It was Papa.
"Papa!" she cried. "I'm here! Here!"
She picked up the cage
and ran toward the sound of his voice.
Timmy followed above her,
stopping now and then to rest upon a stalk.

When she saw Papa at last,
at the edge of the tall grass,
Elsie heard other sounds, too,
for he had bought five hens
and a strutting banty rooster
in town that very day.
He had traded Mama's One Star Quilt for a dog.

How Elsie loved that hound
from the first moment it greeted her,
jumping up and licking her face
and then arooooing in her ear.
She sang back to it, a childhood favorite,
"With a bow-wow here, a bow-wow there . . ."
And Timmy Tune sang along.

That hound, those hens,
that banty rooster,
and all the noise they made
kept Elsie's house full of sound,
and Elsie loved them all
for they turned her house into a true prairie home.

Patricia Lee Gauch, Editor

PHILOMEL BOOKS
A division of Penguin Young Readers Group.   Published by The Penguin Group.
Penguin Group (USA) Inc., 375 Hudson Street, New York, NY 10014, U.S.A.
Penguin Group (Canada), 90 Eglinton Avenue East, Suite 700, Toronto, Ontario M4P 2Y3, Canada (a division of Pearson Penguin Canada Inc.).
Penguin Books Ltd, 80 Strand, London WC2R 0RL, England.
Penguin Ireland, 25 St. Stephen's Green, Dublin 2, Ireland (a division of Penguin Books Ltd).
Penguin Group (Australia), 250 Camberwell Road, Camberwell, Victoria 3124, Australia (a division of Pearson Australia Group Pty Ltd).
Penguin Books India Pvt Ltd, 11 Community Centre, Panchsheel Park, New Delhi - 110 017, India.
Penguin Group (NZ), 67 Apollo Drive, Rosedale, North Shore 0632, New Zealand (a division of Pearson New Zealand Ltd).
Penguin Books (South Africa) (Pty) Ltd, 24 Sturdee Avenue, Rosebank, Johannesburg 2196, South Africa.
Penguin Books Ltd, Registered Offices: 80 Strand, London WC2R 0RL, England.

Design by Semadar Megged.   Text set in 15.5 point Italian Old Style.
The illustrations are rendered in brush & ink with watercolor and pastel.

174-5888

Library of Congress Cataloging-in-Publication Data
Yolen, Jane.   Elsie's bird / Jane Yolen ; illustrated by David Small.   p. cm.
Summary: Young Elsie must find a way to adapt to her new home on the Nebraska prairie after she and her father leave their comfortable city life in Boston.
[1. Prairies—Fiction. 2. Frontier and pioneer life—Nebraska—Fiction. 3. Moving, Household—Fiction. 4. Canaries—Fiction. 5. Loneliness—Fiction.
6. Nebraska—History—Fiction.] I. Small, David, 1945– ill. II. Title.   PZ7.Y78El 2010   [E]—dc22   2009041079
ISBN 978-0-399-25292-1
1 3 5 7 9 10 8 6 4 2